Begin at the Beginning

Amy Schwartz

A Harper Trophy Book

Harper & Row, Publishers

Begin at the Beginning
Copyright © 1983 by Amy Schwartz
All rights reserved. No part of this book may be
used or reproduced in any manner whatsoever without
written permission except in the case of brief
quotations embodied in critical articles and reviews.
Printed in the United States of America.
For information address Harper & Row, Publishers, Inc.,
10 East 53rd Street, New York, N.Y. 10022.
Published simultaneously in Canada by
Fitzhenry & Whiteside Limited, Toronto.

Library of Congress Cataloging in Publication Data
Schwartz, Amy.
  Begin at the beginning.

  Summary: Sara gets stuck when she must paint a picture
for the second grade art show, until she discovers the
best place to begin.
  [1. Painting—Fiction] I. Title.
PZ7.S406Bf 1983   [E]   82-48257
ISBN 0-06-025227-8
ISBN 0-06-025228-6 (lib. bdg.)
ISBN 0-06-443060-X (pbk.)
First Harper Trophy edition, 1984.

For Harte, with thanks

When Sara got home from school, her mother
was in the kitchen baking cookies.
"How was school today, dear?" she asked.

1

"Today," Sara told her mother, "was horrible.
First my clay pot collapsed. Then my toothpick
tree fell apart. And then Miss Weinstein picked me
to do the class painting for the art show tomorrow.
She said she knew I would do something *wonderful*."

"But that *is* wonderful," her mother said.

"No it's not. I don't have even one idea!" Sara said.
"I was going to paint the tree outside my window—
but that's too easy. I have to think of something very
important. I'll get started immediately after this
butter-and-jelly sandwich."

Sara made herself two butter-and-jelly sandwiches,
and ate them piece by piece. Then she ate three
chocolate-covered graham crackers and a pretzel.

"Now," Sara said, "I am ready to begin."

First Sara cleared off her desk. Then she set out
her box of Twenty-Four Very Fine Watercolors
and filled her green glass with water.

She unpacked the fat round brush and the pad
of bright white watercolor paper her grandmother
had given her for Christmas.

Then she sat down to work.

"Now," Sara said, "I am going to paint the most wonderful painting that has ever been painted."

Sara thought for a moment.

"I know: I will paint the earth—and the sky—
and the day and the night, and-the-summer-and-the-
winter-and-everything! I will paint the universe!
Everyone will be amazed."

Sara looked at her blank paper.

"But I wonder where the earth should go,"
she thought.

"Maybe
it should go
here.

"No.
Maybe
it should go
there.

"Maybe
I need another
sandwich."

Twenty minutes later, Sara tried to start again.

"All right," she told herself. "Now. I am going to begin."

She picked up her brush and painted a long blue line. It didn't look right at all. She crumpled up the paper and threw it on the floor.

Sara started one painting after another.

"These paintings are not wonderful at all,"
Sara moaned. "Painting the whole world is harder
than I thought."

"Maybe this paper is too small," she thought.

"Or maybe this brush is too large.

"Maybe twenty-four watercolors are not enough!

"Maybe," thought Sara, "I should change my rinse water."

And she took her green glass into the bathroom.

Sara emptied the water into the sink. She
frowned into the mirror and saw Miss Weinstein
frowning back.

"I am expecting
a *wonderful* painting,
Sara!

"Everyone
is depending
on you!"

Sara's little sister appeared at the door.
"Dinnertime!" she said.
"Thank goodness," Sara sighed.

At the dinner table, everyone had some advice
for Sara.

"You know, Sara, maybe you are trying too hard,"
her father said.

"Or maybe, Sara, you are not trying hard enough,"
her grandmother added.

Soon everyone was talking all at once, waving their forks and spoons in the air.

"Do-it-like-this.." said her father.

"Do-it-like-that.." said her grandmother.

"Do-it-like-this-Sara-do-it-like-that.." chanted her little sister, rocking in her chair.

15

In fact, everyone was so excited that almost no one noticed when Sara pushed her chair away from the table and, leaving her dessert, stomped out of the room.

Sara slammed the door to her room and sat down at her desk. Her paper was still a bright white. The water in her green glass was still clean. Sara still hadn't painted the most wonderful painting that had ever been painted.

Sara sighed a little sigh and put her head on her desk.

When dinner was over, Sara's mother took a square of chocolate cake into Sara's room.

"Oh, Mommy," Sara said. "I was going to paint the earth and the sky and the day and the night, and the summer and the winter and the whole universe. But I can't."

"The universe is *very* big, Sara," her mother said.

Sara and her mother sat together by the window. The sky was just darkening. There was a bit of a bit of a moon.

"Remember, Sara," her mother said, "you can only begin at the beginning."

"But I don't even know where that is," Sara said.

They watched the windows of the houses across the street light up one by one.

"The universe is only people like you and me, and your desk and this room, and those houses..."

"…and the tree outside my window?" Sara asked.

Her mother nodded.

They watched the leaves of the tree rustle in the evening wind.

Sara smiled. "I think I know where to begin now," she said.

Sara's mother gave her a kiss and left her to herself.

Sara pulled her chair up to her desk. She moved her paper a little to the left and a little to the right. She picked up the fat round brush and dipped it in the water in her green glass.

Sara swirled the brush in a tin of deep-brown watercolor, and she began... with her tree.